D0277639

SHORT TALES
Fables

The Lion and the Mouse

Adapted by Shannon Eric Denton
Illustrated by Mike Dubisch

WAYLAND

First published in 2013 by Wayland

Copyright © 2013 Wayland

Wayland
338 Euston Road
London NW1 3BH

Wayland Australia
Level 17/207 Kent Street
Sydney, NSW 2000

Lancashire Library Services	
30118126725898	
PETERS	JF
£8.99	18-Sep-2013
CKl 10/13	

All Rights Reserved.

Adapted Text by Shannon Eric Denton
Illustrations by Mike Dubisch
Colours by Wes Hartman
Edited by Stephanie Hedlund
Interior Layout by Kristen Fitzner Denton and Alyssa Peacock
Book Design and Packaging by Shannon Eric Denton
Cover Design by Alyssa Peacock

Copyright © 2008 by Abdo Consulting Group

A cataloguing record for this title is available at the British Library.
Dewey number: 398.2'452-dc23

Printed in China

ISBN: 978 0 7502 7783 9

Wayland is a division of Hachette Children's Books, an Hachette UK company.
www.hachette.co.uk

One day, a bored mouse was watching a sleeping lion.

The mouse decided it would be fun to surf down the lion.

So the mouse slid down the lion's leg.

Suddenly, the lion woke up
and saw the mouse.

The lion caught the mouse with his paw.

'Please, please let me go!' the mouse begged.

'I'll do anything to pay you back!' the mouse cried.

The lion found the mouse's begging funny.

'Okay, you may go' the lion said.

That afternoon, the lion continued on his way.

He was soon trapped in a hunter's net.

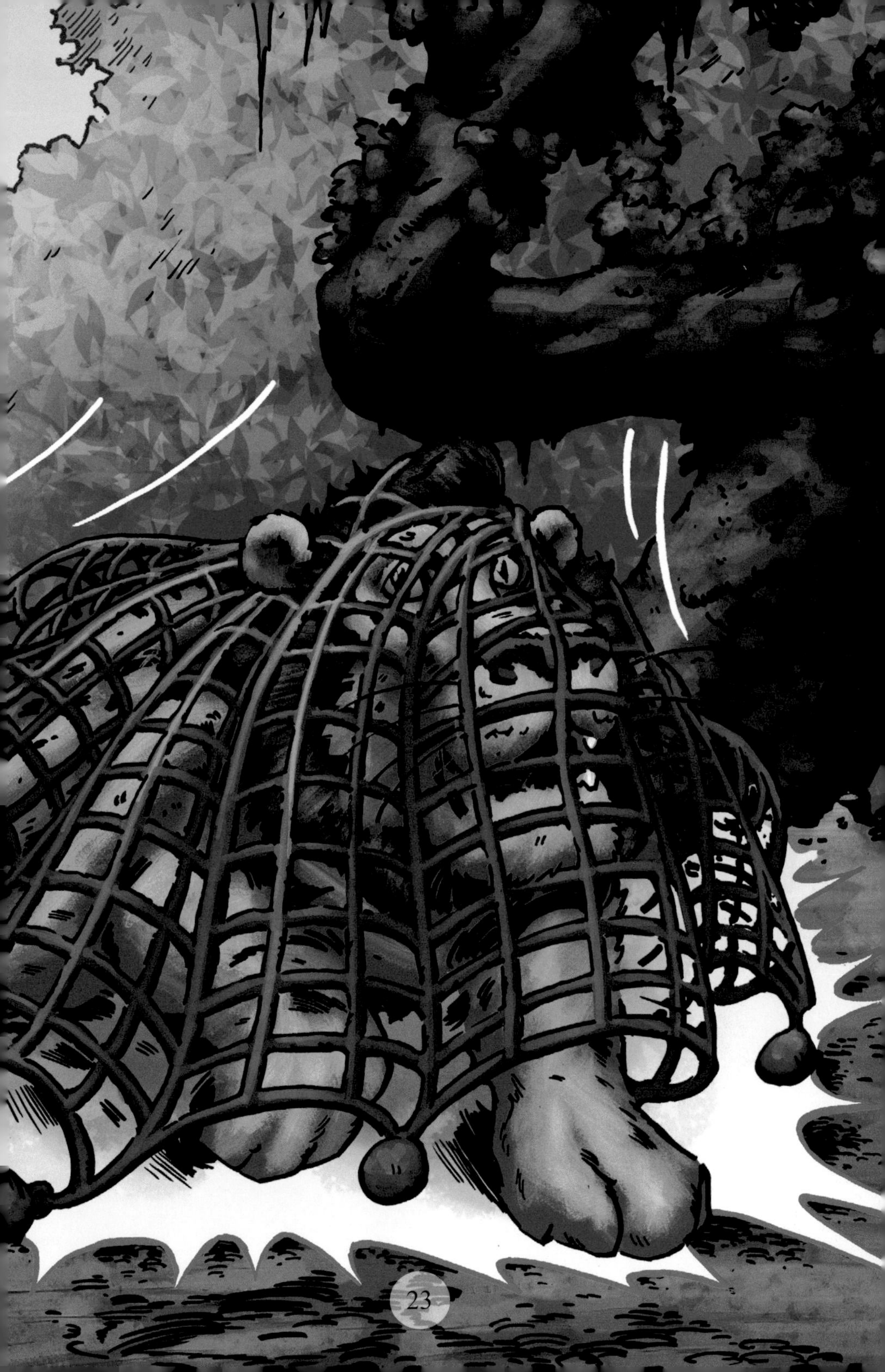

The lion roared his anger,
and the mouse heard him.

The mouse chewed through the ropes and freed the lion.

The lion was surprised the
mouse had freed him.

Together, the lion and his new friend walked away.

The moral of the story is:

Little friends may prove to be great friends.

SHORT TALES
Fairy Tales

Titles in the Short Tales Fairy Tales series:

Aladdin and the Lamp

978 0 7502 7750 1

Beauty and the Beast

978 0 7502 7752 5

Jack and the Beanstalk

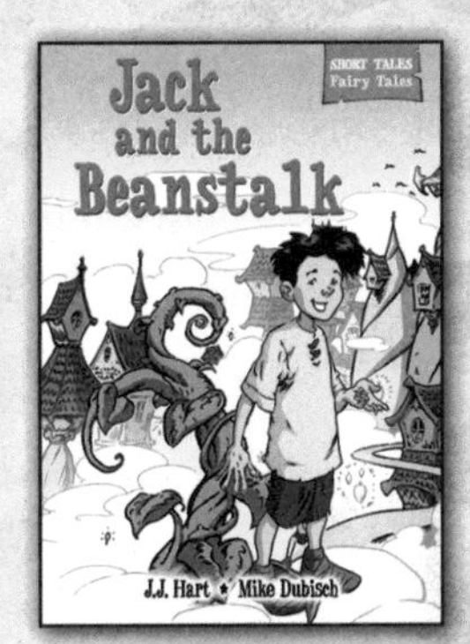

978 0 7502 7751 8

Puss in Boots

978 0 7502 7754 9

Sleeping Beauty

978 0 7502 7755 6

The Little Mermaid

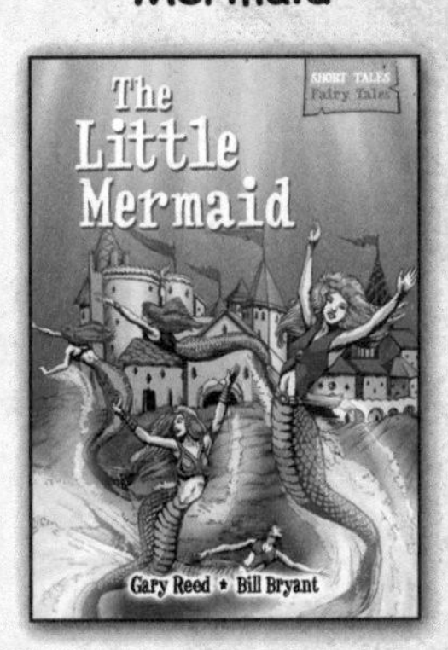

978 0 7502 7753 2

WAYLAND

www.waylandbooks.co.uk

Follow us on Twitter @waylandbooks | Find us on Facebook Wayland Books

SHORT TALES
Fables

Titles in the Short Tales Fables series:

The Ants and the Grasshopper

978 0 7502 7756 3

The Boy Who Cried Wolf

978 0 7502 7757 0

The Fox and the Grapes

978 0 7502 7758 7

The Lion and the Mouse

978 0 7502 7783 9

The Tortoise and the Hare

978 0 7502 7784 6

The Town Mouse and the Country Mouse

978 0 7502 7785 3

WAYLAND

www.waylandbooks.co.uk

Follow us on Twitter @waylandbooks | Find us on Facebook Wayland Books